DESIRE: A HAUNTING

Molly Gaudry

praise for
Desire: A Haunting

"Even alone, writes Molly Gaudry, 'we are not unloved.' And indeed, a reader cannot help but be trapped in tentacles of love when reading her twisting, tender *Desire: A Haunting*. No one but Gaudry paints language with so much care, with so much lonely, heart-dreamed beauty. No one else paints scars so naked and so necessary. This book is a breathing thing, a piece of life-in-love-in-art." — Amber Sparks, author of *The Unfinished World and Other Stories*

"Each page is an epiphany of spectral nesting dolls: open love to expose lamentation; crack the soft skeleton of memory to release matriarchal debt — and hidden inside it all, Gaudry's spare lyric floats through us, ethereal and elegant." — Lily Hoang, author of *A Bestiary*

"This book is more poem than most poems — ghosts — literary and created — populating a prose broken into savage and sweet lines — hands drawn through viscera and the appearance thereof — to concoct a drama as yet untold yet retold a thousand times over: love love love love love, I love you I love you. Molly Gaudry is our Neruda, our Marquez, our chronicler of times spent and as yet foretold." — Jamie Iredell, author of *Last Mass*

"With the sharpest of knives, Molly Gaudry carves richness and poverty, sadness and sweetness, violence and love into the reader's consciousness. A cut neck, a suicide, a drowning, you want to look away, but you don't, because you would miss your chance to live. *Desire: A Haunting* is a perfect, tender book." — Amina Cain, author of *Creature*

"*Desire: A Haunting* is a novel broken into lines, & this breakage uses the space of the page to enact the blank spaces of myth & the fantastic, of memory & desire. The narrator asserts that 'sometimes we are powerless against our passions,' yet in the book power matures in passion's interstices, makes sense of trauma & develops it into strength. This is a delightful, unsettling & addictive book in which the dead speak to & follow the living, in which memory knots into presence, in which love is always a ghost." — Mathias Svalina, author of *Destruction Myth for you*

Ampersand Books
www.ampersand-books.com

ISBN: 978-0-9861370-3-7
First Ampersand Books edition

Cover design: Jana Vukovic
Interior design: Matthew Revert

DESIRE: A HAUNTING

"It is in a house that one is alone."

—Marguerite Duras

"But I am not alone. I have you."

—Lydia Millet

prologue

before the first soft light of day

I am undressed and in the water

                              with every stroke

I stretch

reach

pull toward my heart

and push away behind me

some memory of you

how you love to have the tea house trimmed

with yellow lights all winter long

how you light a candle in every window as if to

say

          OH COME ALL YE FAITHFUL

1

but I am not joyful

my only triumph today

is I have risen before dawn and forced my body

into water

where there is nothing but water to feel

I do this because I can't stand to open my eyes

in the cottage

to see so clearly morning streaming through

curtains

as if nothing happened here

every day I remove myself from bed

grope in the dark

hold my breath to keep from screaming all the

way from the last step of the back porch to just

past the cherry blossoms

                         even the cherry blossoms

remind me

I have been trying to write

                    more than anything

I want my voice to ring true to you when I say I

am trying to stay positive

                    with every word

I fail

on my back now

floating

I let my arms and shoulders rest

watch the sun rise over the sea

over me

kick my way slowly back to shore

tired and numb

the way I need to be to start each day

                    and still she is waiting

                       all winter long

since Christmas

she has been waiting

                       every morning

when I return from my swim

she is waiting

standing

on the back porch

arms outstretched

saying YOU CAN'T IGNORE ME FOREVER

part one

THE COTTAGE

she stalks me at night when I take out the cans

    says YOU WILL DIE A VIRGIN UNLESS

YOU FIND SOMEONE TO TAKE OUT YOUR

TRASH FOR YOU

the air is damp

                              her voice is thin with rasp

          are you in pain

          she nods BUT WHAT CAN YOU DO

I make borage soup

one pound pheasant confit from the winter

pantry

skinned

shredded

skin fried and saved for sandwiches

two quarts broth

two cups soaked grass peas

one diced red onion

two generous hands full

torn young borage leaves

there was always fresh borage at the tea house

                      we used its stems as stirrers

to flavor certain beverages

its leaves for Frittelle Di Borragine and

Ligurian Pansotti

                      we used its flowers

to garnish blackberry ginger granita

add color to our cucumber and dill cream

cheese sandwiches

from which it was my job to cut the crusts

                      we froze them in ice spheres

for blueberry mint and pink and lavender

lemonades

after I had been at the tea house for some time

Sam taught me to place those tiny blue

blossoms atop his chilled Marcona Almond &

Poblano Chile Soup

                              when it was ready

my task was to spoon it over his perfectly

molded tower of Spanish Sherry Crab Salad

layered with mashed avocado and lime

further layered with diced watermelon

crumbled feta

finely chopped mint

winters

we used the flowers for borage honey ice
cream

your favorite

served with honey glazed walnuts

drizzled with warm borage honey

I prefer simpler meals here in the cottage

although I still make infusions with bruised

fresh borage leaves when I have a sore throat

                      I steep its stems in my wine

dry its leaves for the calming tea you taught me

to make from violet and hawthorn and linden

                      I use its leaves for poultices

to relieve insect bites and stings

and to soothe dry skin

she has gone so long without water her mouth
skin is cracking

lie on the floor
close your eyes

I drape the poultice over her
affected areas and she reaches for my hand for
reassurance
when she doesn't find it
she lowers her back to the ground

she spends the night there

eyes still closed when I leave for my morning

swim

when I return

she is waiting on the porch

                she follows me into the cottage

and watches as I sweep the borage from the

floorboards into a bin

     DO YOU REMEMBER ME

I boil rosebuds for the salve you taught me to
make

           I stir until their petaled fists unfurl

in the iron kettle over our fire

to fill the silence

I share a story Sam told me about a man who
died in a duel

        a spear went through the man's throat
                            after that

he was always searching for water

        I put a straw in a glass of water for her
place it on the table

          her broken lips go to the straw
and she pretends to drink

pretends to understand

         I pretend not to understand her
pretending

        we are like children playing cards

after dinner

when the salve has cooled

I pretend to dab a bit into one cracked corner of

her mouth

she says I ALREADY FELT BETTER AFTER

THAT POULTICE

hold still anyway

I dab the other corner of her mouth

my finger making circles in the air

there now

feels better

doesn't it

                    she smashes her lips together

smiles

later that night she reaches to shoo a fly from

my glass

                    her hand goes right through it

through the gold lip of the green cut glass

through the wine

through the borage leaves steeping in my wine

through the bright blue flower floating on top

and through the fly that does not budge

when I learn her favorite color is lemon

I scrub the cottage with it until I am numb

she calls me DUMB WOMAN

either because I am silent

or she doesn't care if we are clean

I do

she tells me her name was Pearl among the living but those days are gone and it is too tiring to retrieve them

        she says CALL ME OGIE

IT HAS A CERTAIN TONE TO IT

LIKE OGRE

JUST NOT AS MONSTROUS

        she flashes her teeth and says I PROMISE

I WON'T EAT YOU

I tell her she may call me dog

she snorts WHAT KIND OF NAME IS

THAT

it's how my mother called me

BUT WHAT DID THEY CALL YOU AT THE

OTHER PLACE

the dressmaker's daughter

as in THIS IS THE DRESSMAKER'S

DAUGHTER

YOU KNOW

THE ONE WHO

29

                       then their voices failed

and they gestured meaningfully

busying themselves with tasks or other topics

of conversation so that I was left to relive the

rest of the sentence alone

I head for the door

going for a swim

don't wait up

she follows me to the beach and says SO

WE BOTH HAVE MOTHER SCARS TO BEAR

I remove my veil

lift and raise my dress over my head

LISTEN

I plunge in

to my knees

thighs

hips

waist

drowning the sound of her voice in waves

THEY'RE DEAD she shouts

I stretch and reach

WE ARE ALL THAT'S LEFT

I pull my body forward

SO WHAT IF YOU'RE UNTOUCHED AND

I'M UNTOUCHABLE

I push her and the shore away

WE ARE NOT UNLOVED

Ogie wakes me in the morning

                              for the first time

I've slept past sunrise

          she stands over me and says she's

BELOW THE WEATHER

IN NEED OF MEAT AND SEX

she had twelve children

                  her husband and their six sons

and depending if the last girl lived or died their

five or six daughters

all survived her in a city far away

                  she admits that anymore

she does not think of them often

but today is the anniversary of her death

which was so long ago even her great-

grandchildren have grown old and died

in the kitchen I put a new straw in a fresh glass
of water for her and tell her if I could I would
find them all and ask them here and hold them
for her because I am sinew and she is ancient as
trees

over time I learn her husband was a merchant

in that city far away

                  the family prospered there

but it is to the solitude of this seaside cottage

far removed from the rest of town that she feels

bound

and to her childhood here

with her mother

even after all these years Ogie is still unable to

accept that she is the only ghost in this cottage

she continues to wait

one day she says ONE OF MOTHER'S

FAVORITE THINGS TO SAY TO ME WAS —

LEAVE ME BE ELSE I SHALL SHUT THEE

INTO THE DARK CLOSET!

she gestures toward the closet behind me

where your needle lace wedding dress rests

where Mother's large red cloak hangs

SHE NEVER DID

IT WAS JUST A THREAT TIRED MOTHERS

SOMETIMES MAKE

as my own mother died here

with her mother who died here

I tell her I understand

but Ogie turns inwardly during her sadnesses

makes jokes instead

      I say *I know*

      it must be hard

to love so much still

one morning when I come in from my swim

she asks me to follow her and leads me into the

forest

under a giant tree

she once buried a stone chicken to its cheeks

I unearth it for her and carry it home

at her command

I smash it to bits with a hammer in the shed

on scraps of paper

I tie to each sacrificial hunk

I write our inheld grievances

WHERE ARE YOU

why haven't you written

from the farthest tip of our tiny peninsula

I throw them into the sea

we watch

until the final ripple dissolves in waves

inside

I put out our fire

                              our day is done

and still I am thinking of you

the evening you wore your nightblack wings

a specific Halloween

and before that

a different night

the straps of your gray silk slip falling away

beneath my fingers

my palms

the scent of jasmine in your room

                              I am in your room

          I have knocked and entered your room

and we are wrapped around each other on the

bed over the wet floor where a water glass lies

broken and a dead man watches

astonished

as we kiss

to get away sometimes

I go for long walks

alone

in the forest

                    I know don't have to ask Ogie

to leave me be

but I do

this morning

like every morning when I swim

she watches from the back porch

                       she doesn't like me to go

into the water but we both know I swim less

recklessly when she is watching

very early in our acquaintance she tried to keep

me from my routine by demanding I take her

into town

     she commanded me to HITCH THE

WHEELS

                             I felt burdened

tired too

but we needed meat and manicotti shells in any

case

she thinks it is important for me to get out of

the cottage

even if I do put up a fight

last time we went to town she lifted her dress

and mooned every video camera in the Savings

& Loan

for some reason this disturbed the time

and temperature display and they have still not

figured out how to fix it

either to reward her or thank her

I treat us to an ice water at the diner

                              I ask for two straws

one so I can drink

one so Ogie can pretend to drink

       tiny and miserable on the red plastic

booth beside me she says IT'S BEEN AN AGE

SINCE I COULD EAT OR DRINK

the waiter comes to refill and stare at me so

many times I have to finally tell him to stop

                      when he leaves

I lift the edge of my veil

let the straw touch my lips

and I drink

             even though I am not thirsty

I drink the water for Ogie

on our way home

we pass the church

            I beg her to hold my hand

and walk with me down the altar so we can

pretend to be our mothers and give them each

a happy wedding day at last

                     that night

we light paper lanterns

            we release them into the sea

our lemon balm and sage is ready to harvest

                                                I need sugar

cornstarch

butter

eggs

        I ask Ogie to come with me into town
because I don't like to go by myself

                            with her beside me

I am not so alone

                              they can't see her

do the things she does to try and make me feel
less alone

        they can't see my lips twitch into smile
behind my veil

the store owner pretends to watch the new

checkout girl but really she is watching

me

                              for the first time

I speak to her

          when you were a little girl

were you my mother's friend

          she says I DON'T THINK SO

                    Ogie lets out a huff beside me

                              on our way home

I tell her

          I didn't want to know anyway

            I just thought it might be nice

to hear a story

or a rumor

to have some sighting of my past that isn't

mine

at the door of the old prison

I pluck a red rose

just as I always do

                          I pretend to hand it to Ogie

and she stands tall

pretending to hold it as I hold it for her

                      we do not speak of my mistake

of speaking in town

after groceries are unloaded

we make our way into the forest

                              saturated in birdsong

shrouded in a faint fog

we cross paths with a partridge and her brood

                                    a squirrel

tosses down a nut to us and wakes a sleeping

fox

we pass the afternoon like this

                when we are ready to turn back

I notice how beautifully Ogie shines in the

sunbeams bursting from the tangled shadows

of the treetop canopy over our hard-packed

dirt path home

in a saucepan I whisk five eggs

six yolks

two cups sugar until smooth

                              in a bowl

I whisk a quarter cup and two tablespoons

cornstarch with a cup of lemon juice to create a

slurry

                    I whisk the slurry into the egg mix

                         I add one cup fresh sage leaves

                              I eat a sage leaf

and Ogie pretends to eat a sage leaf

                         once the mixture is thick

I whisk in two sticks butter

transfer it all back into the bowl

set the bowl in the icebox to chill

after my morning swim

I pick out the sage leaves by hand

      I spend over an hour scraping the curd

from the underside of each leaf

working along each vein with the serrated edge

of a grapefruit spoon

                  Ogie pretends

with a pretend spoon of her own

to work her veins too

      have you ever tried curd

                she shakes her head

      then tomorrow I'll make biscuits and you

can try it then

we used to eat biscuits and curd every day for
lunch

                  you sat in the kitchen
with Sam and me and spooned the curd onto
seven steaming biscuits straight from the oven
two each for us and three for Sam

               the memory catches in my throat

     of course
if you don't like it
you can have rose petal and lemon balm jelly instead

finally we have collected enough dried rose

petals from the roses I have brought back from

the prison

                                            I add them

to the lemon balm leaves already dried from

the garden

                              after they've boiled

and steeped an hour

I strain the liquid through a sieve into a

saucepan

add lemon juice

whisk in pectin and sugar

and boil

until the last grain of sugar disappears

Ogie stands beside me by the fire

                she fingers one of the elastics

I wear around my wrist for my hair and her

finger goes right through it

right through my wrist

     I WAS BORN IN THAT PRISON she says

BUT YOU KNEW THAT

     yes

I transfer the reduced jelly into sterile jars

        Ogie's hand goes from my wrist

to the rose on the table

           she pretends

to ruffle the edges of its petals

      I WAS ASKED ONCE WHO MY FATHER

WAS

      I SHOULD HAVE ANSWERED GOD

ALMIGHTY BUT I SAID I HAD NO FATHER

      I SAID MOTHER HAD PLUCKED ME FROM

A ROSE BUSH

I BELIEVED IT TOO

THAT I WAS A RED ROSE

A FLOWER

    after a long silence she asks PLEASE for
another glass of water

                I set one on the table
and tell her I would give anything for her to be
able to drink the water or to taste the curd
to be able to satisfy her thirst
              but her mind is elsewhere

    SOMETIMES I STILL LIKE TO THINK IT

that night I hear her voice through the walls

THE MOST COMMON WOOD USED IN

ITALY FOR PANEL PAINTINGS COMES FROM

POPLARS

SLIGHTLY YELLOW

BUT GENERALLY WHITE

then she says MONA LISA IS SO SAD

LIKE WATER

SNAP YOUR FINGERS FOR ME

I KNEW HER ONCE BUT MY EYES ARE

BAD

I go to her but all I can do is nod and shush as

I pretend to hold her hand as she pretends to

hold my hand

                              I do not understand

but the least someone can do when a loved one

talks is listen

in the dark

Ogie tells me how she died

she says she was thrown from a boat

that collided with another and exploded

MAYBE TOO THICK FOG OR A

MISCALCULATION

she washed onshore of our little peninsula and
caught a fish but could not bring herself to kill
it after watching one small gill quiver

THAT POOR BEAST GASPING FOR AIR

NO

WE WOULD NOT BOTH DIE FROM DROWNING

not recognizing her own land

she attempted to forage for berries on what she

thought was an island

      BUT EVEN THE GRAPES WERE THIN AND

BROWN THAT YEAR

in a fit of extreme hunger

several nights later

she was lifted high by a blizzard of birds and

set down on the roof of this cottage

which she sank through

straight into the attic

where she lived for many years

a new woman

happy to be reinstated in her own familiar

cottage where she not so happily observed the

daily habits of my great-grandparents and their

daughter Susan

no matter how loudly Ogie screamed

or wailed

trying to spook them

they did not hear

in a different version

Ogie claims she died wearing muslin

pantaloons

a martyr

having devoted her life to lepers

whom she tended lovingly after their flesh

turned unbearable

she kept them clean

wiped their bodies of themselves

held their hands when they ascended beyond

pain

AUTHORITIES WANTED TO ERECT A

STATUE IN MY HONOR

BUT I TOLD THEM IF THEY DID I'D HAVE IT

TORN DOWN

EVEN IF I HAD TO DO IT MYSELF

SO SELFLESS I WAS

DURING MY YEARS AMONG THE LIVING

I go to church because I love how dark it is

inside

how I can focus on just one votive light

its pull on me

and feel my body leaning forward

almost unafraid

after church

I always go to the market-place for milk and

eggs

                                      Ogie meets me there

                      the deal is she keeps me company

then we go home

unload

and I take her into the forest

once

on our way home

I showed her the pew where I pray

                                                I told her how

from that spot I have the best view of the

saints' faces in the glass

                          her reaction was eyes rolled up

and mouth shut tight

today she walks right through a woman

squeezing oranges

and I have to laugh when the woman jumps a

little and drops them

                        the woman turns and stares

hard at me

                              I pick up the oranges

and hold them out to her

                        when she doesn't take them

I purchase them myself

even though we have more oranges and

marmalade at home than I know what to do

with

so I make candied oranges

the way Sam taught me

                    I cut the thinnest slices I can

place them into a saucepan

fill with cold water

boil

drain

return the slices to the pan

cover with cold water

and boil

before turning down the heat and simmering

until the peels are tender

I remove them once again

return them to the saucepan

mix in corn syrup

sugar

water

and heat until the sugar dissolves

                              I add the orange slices

simmer

until the peel is translucent

until the syrup has reduced

then lift the slices one by one and set them on a

wire rack to dry

I remember Sam telling me that waiting for

them to dry was his favorite part

at least four hours of waiting

that waiting is always the best part

Ogie assumes I was fed from a bottle

                                              I tell her no

I remember Mother's lips on mine

breath-wilted rose petals pushed against my

tongue

dust in the air sparkling in morning sun from

the windows

pine-fresh floors

the two of us on trains

the comfort-smell of boiled peanuts

applause from the tent

and us with the elephants and horses

fixing the costumes for their sequined lady

riders

I remember warmth on Mother's cot and

looking at photographs from a book she

guarded carefully throughout our travels

SHADOW MEMORIES you called them

many days later I find your letter

stuck between the floorboards of the porch

$$\text{by its date}$$

I see you sent it some time ago

you wrote there had been a fire

but nothing damaged that couldn't be mended

or replaced

you said sometimes you thought of Zepha

but not too often

just every once in a while

when the wind picked up

you included a string of ten numbers and said

the fire had been a good excuse to wire the tea

house for a telephone and that the earpiece

and mouthpiece of the pink receiver were gold

and for some reason that gold reminded you of

me at the store and if I should ever like to call

sometime you would like that very much

Ogie finds me on the porch

WHAT'S WITH YOU

YOU LOOK LIKE YOU'RE MAD OR

SOMETHING

for a long time I stare down Prison Lane

toward town

                                             I go inside

pour myself a glass of wine

then another

and another

in the morning Ogie tells me I missed the
fireworks

THEY WERE SPECTACULAR

IF YOU HADN'T BEEN OUT COLD YOU

WOULD HAVE SEEN THEM LIGHT UP THE SEA

LIKE THE SISTINE CHAPEL

YOUR LOSS

NOT MINE

I cook a fish one night for dinner

                    a deep death smell lingers

for days

                              luckily

it is cool outside

so we open all the windows

ask the air to do its work

on the second day

Ogie begins to hold her nose and makes

retching noises

on the third day

I move out of my room and into the attic so I

can sleep again

                                        that night

I hear a bump through the wall and answer

Montreal

Ogie relays this to me in the morning

                        we still have no idea

what that was all about

Ogie comes out of the cottage to sit beside me

on the sand

where I am attempting to bronze my flesh

the last of the sun

shines through her body

the curve of her long neck glows bright

hidden in night

I lean toward her

touch her knee with my knee

feel chilled

my eyes water when she wiggles her ears

trying to make me laugh

at midnight mass

alone

I listen to the sounds of wind and rain on

darkened stained-glass faces

                              the smell of damp bodies

huddled together

musky and warm

inside the hushed church

seeking hope and solace

makes me feel as if I have turned good

                              I pray for Ogie

I pray for her soul

for mine

my only friend is a ghost

who keeps me company because she feels

bound to me

or to the cottage

and because without me to see or hear her

she doesn't exist

she is smiling at me today

happy watching me in the patch as I fill my

basket with so many berries we will have

preserves enough for winter and spring

and possibly summer too

she says she was taught to draw in that city far

away and asks if I was taught to draw

       I tell her I can't think of a single reason

why I would have ever been taught to draw

      she sets her face like steel and says

THERE'S NO REASON TO GET ALL HOT

      I WAS ONLY ASKING BECAUSE

THESE DAYS ARE TOO SLOW AND WE NEED

SOMETHING TO FILL UP ALL THIS EMPTY AIR

we sit beside each other

        as she moves her hand over the paper

before her

I copy her hand's motions with mine

and move my chalk against the paper before

me

        at one point she leans over

cups the back of her hand inside the palm of

my hand

and I can almost feel us touching

        in this way

we pass the most of autumn

by winter

we have several stacks of stark naked nudes to

show for our efforts

                              their shadowed lines

and curves are piled

one atop another

the sound outside of a twig cracking

I turn to listen

it is getting colder

soon

it will be time for our final harvest

MERRY CHRISTMAS Ogie says

I set out a glass of water for her

Merry Christmas Ogie

OR SHOULD I SAY HAPPY

ANNIVERSARY

I raise my glass and say *yes*

to us

a year ago

my first Christmas here

I lit a candle in the window

walked slowly to the closet door

felt a shock run up my neck when I opened

it and touched the hem of the sleeve of your

needle lace wedding dress

I ran my thumb along Mother's red cloak

overwhelmed by the smell of roses

                I ruffled the rows and rows

of rose petals she had sewn flat like sequins

      IT'S STUNNING

ISN'T IT

who's there

CAN YOU HEAR ME

yes

who's there

YOU CAN HEAR ME

I HAVE BEEN WAITING SO LONG

DON'T BE AFRAID

I KNEW YOUR MOTHER

AND SOMETIMES IF I WAILED REALLY LOUD

SHE COULD HEAR ME TOO

CAN YOU SEE ME

I WON'T HURT YOU

I'LL STAY RIGHT HERE

DO YOU REMEMBER ME

tonight

I have prepared for Ogie the meals you made

for me and Sam every Christmas

                                                   first

I present her with roasted acorn squash seeds

then honey-roasted figs with basil and goat

cheese

grilled radishes with rosemary brown butter

chocolate balsamic roasted beets

maple glazed roasted carrots

lamb chops with garlic mint sauce

throughout it all

Ogie pretends to smell

she sniffs and says TRULY

YOU HAVE OUTDONE YOURSELF

COME HERE AND GIVE ME A HUG

I tell her to cut it out

I light a candle in the window

add another log to our fire

                              after my fourth glass

I go to the closet and open the door

and there they are

your needle lace wedding dress

Mother's red cloak

Ogie jokingly pulls it off its hanger and

says YOUR CLOAK MADAM

I stare at the hanger still swinging on the rod

                         I look down at her hands

at the cloak she is holding in her hands

she flings it away

and I catch it in midair

     the petals feel like wet satin in my fists

       one bright red petal comes loose

rises briefly between us

settles on the floor

Ogie stares at the petal

I stare at her

at her hands

pick it up

she shakes her head

try

please

for me

she gets down to her knees

first one

then the other

still staring at the petal

                          she reaches out one finger

pokes

the petal slides across the floor

I lift the cloak to her shoulders

hold it open

put it on

she turns her back to me

steps into it

easy as the living

I drape the collar around her neck and it hangs

loosely around her torso

                                          too big

it falls from one shoulder

I find Mother's sewing basket

her thread

                        Ogie hands me her petal

                                on the floor

I sew it to the hem of her dress with one small

cross stitch

it stays

even as she walks around the room

kicking her skirt dramatically

it stays

                              if I couldn't see her

it would look like a winter drift swirling

coming in from under the door

and tossing a single red petal around the room

I get to work altering the cloak so it will fit

                                                                 when I am done

I slip it over her shoulders

                                                                 once more

the fabric drapes tenderly around her body

for the first time we are able to wrap our arms

around each other

but delicately

careful not to damage petals

I feel the pressure of my hands on her back

        I rest my cheek against her shoulder

and feel held

so close I swear I can feel the warmth of her

which of course reminds me of the warmth of

you

and Mother too

as if in a trance

Ogie fingers the petals of the cloak

        I NEVER THOUGHT I'D BE ABLE TO

TOUCH ANYTHING EVER AGAIN

to celebrate

I present her with her Christmas gift

a gold-rimmed water goblet that I promise to

keep filled at all times

                                                 she tells me

my gift is in the attic

and we go upstairs to find it

                                    in a tiny gold frame

a photograph of me and Mother and

Grandmother

taken one night before they died

                                              behind us

a bright sunburst shaped like Ogie

part two

THE FOREST

since Christmas

Ogie has been debating a departure

the cloak has given her courage

she feels stronger with it on

she is ready to leave

to search for her mother

she plans to go to that city far away

where perhaps there are new trails or clues

> through the screen door

she beckons me inside

    IT'S TIME

    don't go

    IN CASE I DON'T MAKE IT BACK

NEVER FEAR DEATH

    IT'S LIKE WAKING FROM A DREAM

    YOU DON'T REMEMBER MUCH ABOUT

YOUR LIFE

A FEW DETAILS

BUT YOU KNOW IT FELT REAL WHEN YOU

WERE THERE

please

LISTEN

YOU HAVE GROWN TOO THIN BECAUSE OF

ME BECAUSE YOU PRETEND TO EAT SO I CAN

PRETEND TO BE EATING

I HAVE BEEN TWISTING MY FINGERS ALL

NIGHT AND I HAVE DECIDED

IT IS DECIDED

Ogie is not one to leave ceremoniously

she leaves

she is gone

my first night in the cottage without her

I make a cup of tea and strangle the bag

                    I touch the boiling water

        I dip my hand in a blue mixing bowl

filled with ice water

make violent waves that lap against its harbor

                        I make up voices

    I'm so green

    I'm so seasick

    I'm so drunk

    please

save us from all this water

Ogie liked to watch me as I carved meat

        she liked to watch me grate cheese

and garnish our plates with radish stars and

tomato roses

        when she stopped sitting with me

in the kitchen I should have realized something

was wrong

one afternoon I found her tucked into the

branches of a tamarack mouthing strange

enchantments

rituals I could not understand

                    rarely did she enter the forest

without me

                        I should have known

                        I should have seen

                    she was getting braver

testing her resolve and strength

declaring her independence from me and from

the cottage

when I was young

I spent my days forming clusters of stones for

no reason

                        I did this obsessively

unable to stop

I am trying to say I understand why Ogie left

                         sometimes we are powerless

against our passions

our obsessions

                                 we have no choice

but leave

in the months following

I cut slivers into all my meat

                    I slide clean coins inside

               I had stopped eating meat

long before she left

but I continue to prepare it as offerings for the

dead

the wolves come and I help them deliver their

young

if not drunk then getting there

        I like a little twist with my grain

so rub the rind on the rim please

                thanks

on Ogie's birthday

I celebrate without her

                         in her honor

I say a few words not about death

      all day I play with her old doll out back

beneath the falling cherry blossoms

                      I wash and comb

and attempt to curl the doll's hair

but the best I can manage is a frizzle

      I place her gently on a bed of branches

layer her in fallen blossom

          I leave her closed eyes uncovered

deep in the forest one night

I see a horror frozen in a block of ice smooth as
tile

a snow image in a seaweed headdress

the snow around us is flat

no footprints

      the snow image's eyes are pointed down

and in her open palm a pile of stars glows like

embers in ash

                  I have a bit of oil with me

sealed in a feed tin

so I stoke a fire with my mouth

                        in our darkness

surrounded by snow

I work through the night

in the morning

the blue sky opens wide above us

                when I have melted the ice

I wrap the snow image in my arms

     give me your pain

     I can take it

     I will take it

the snow image is my cure for lonely nights

        I have two mouths to feed again

      I visit her throughout the day with food

and she stays in the yard where I put her

           she does not leave

I adorn her in dresses from Mother's crates

I string a necklace of petunias

for her to wrap around her neck like pearls

once

I tried to bring her inside

                                 her throat swelled

                                       I watched

helpless

as her face turned blue

as she exhaled and filled the room like a

balloon with so many ghosts of children they

piled up to the roof and scattered down dust

from the ceiling fan

naked as cherubs and singing in rhymes

a boy shows up from Blackwell's Farm on

the other side of town and presents my snow

image with a glass eye

in turn

she warns me

DO NOT WEAR ANY APRONS THIS YEAR

sure enough

all winter long

we find one animal after another strung up by

its hindquarters

left to die

in the spring

a colorful flowering covers their corpses like a

throw

then one morning

as if attempting to break free

Ogie's face appears in my bedroom window

                        she mimes with both hands

pressed flat against the pane

first one

then the other

testing every corner and edge

her expression alarmed and comical

I open the door and see at her waist a small boy
whose throat is sliced open

Ogie gives me a squeeze and says
YOU'RE HAMMERED

who's this

WILLIAM

did you find--

she shakes her head

ARE YOU GOING TO HELP HIM OR NOT

I wash what used to be his flesh

     I sew it back together with Mother's thread

          when I am finished

William pretends to take off his bloody clothes

          Ogie pretends

on the other side of the tub

to bathe him

so I too pretend to bathe him

          when we are done

he stands

     he raises his arms to be picked up

I hesitate

just for a moment

then reach under his armpits

                he rises into the air

                    he is floating

pretending to be held

            so I pretend to lift him

over the lip of the tub

and he descends to the floor

where I put him

that night while he is sleeping in Mother's bed

on his side

his hands in prayer beneath his head

I find in a different crate a dress made from

tiny yellow flowers that I cut apart at the seams

and begin to refashion into a neat suit

                                  Ogie wants to help

so I teach her to string a strand of petunia

petals

                         she drapes it over his neck

a lei

a snake

to hide his scar

in the morning

William is awake and peeping sideways at me

from the edge of my bed

I ask if he is hungry

he nods and says I MISS PEACHES

when we leave the cottage

he reaches up

slips a hand into each of our hands

                                              in this way

we make our journey into town

at the market-place we search for the ripest
peach

         I bite into it

then reach down and place the broken piece

inside his open mouth

    it falls to the ground between his feet

but he savors it

eyes closed

chewing slowly

        swallowing at last

he wipes his lips with the back of his hand

looks up

  asks PLEASE for more

inevitably they fall in love

young William preferring for Ogie and not me

to bathe him before bed

                                  he kisses her cheek

before turning toward the wall and burrowing

into the child-sized bedcovers I made from a

dress of blue hydrangeas

one morning he wakes us early and leads Ogie

in a lively dance that slithers into the yard

and ends under the cherry blossoms that fall

all around us as we march unevenly to the

soundless beat of his made-up snare drum

his little belly sticks out

in front and his little hands wave invisible

drumsticks

Ogie swings her arms and kicks her legs

attempting to teach me the Charleston

eventually she gives up

delights William instead with the intricacies of

the bees knees

after dinner

after several drinks while they are sleeping

I take a long walk and find myself on the shore

of our little peninsula

desirous of something unnamable and fighting

desperately

the urge to pitch myself in

at the water's edge my body stiffens

       I begin to regret how much I drank

I close my eyes

tip my chin toward the sky as black as I have

ever seen it

and lose all resolve

a spray of sea water settles on my face

like dust

I strip

slip into the water

easy as an eel

        I remember your many blends of teas

and the scents of all those different wildflowers

you foraged for and brought back to the tea

house to tie with purple twine into fat bushels

that you asked me help you hang upside down

to dry in the darkest corner of the cellar

in the middle of the night William gasps

chokes on sobs

                I spill red wine on my collar

              Ogie gathers him in her arms

carries him to her recliner

                 she rocks him back to sleep

I wake to find them lifted into the air by a

swarm of butterflies

                              they hover above me

like two sailors sharing a hammock

                              I reach to shake Ogie

                                        slowly

as if they are on a paper ship

fragile and waterlogged

on the verge of sinking

                    I step up and pull their bodies

out of the wings of creatures

                         William lets out a whimper

and in the morning we are all slightly terrified

heavy with worry every night Ogie shuffles to

the room where William sleeps

                              she reassures herself

with a light touch of her single rose petal to his

forehead

he is safe

tonight

instead of returning to her recliner

she sits near me and begins to sing a strange

tune

                    when I ask what it is

she raises her shoulders

holds up her hands

I JUST LOVE HIS LITTLE HANDS

absorbed in the mysteries of Mother's crates

I am organizing her fabrics and materials onto

open shelves for easier access

come here a moment

I want to test this vine

DON'T YOU LIKE MY LITTLE VERSO-

SONGO

I DON'T KNOW WHY I'M REMEMBERING

IT NOW

AFTER ALL THIS TIME

lovely

now twirl

the vine falls to the ground around her like a
lasso

      you hold it now
take it from me
      twirl again and lift it up

            she spins and it rises slowly
wrapping her in a loose coil

Easter morning

        I place a basket of chocolate bunnies

at the foot of William's bed

                Ogie wakes

says her sinuses are acting up

declines to go to mass with me

but for hushed voices murmuring prayers

all is silence

                      I shape my hand into a cup

scoop a fistful of holy water

let it trickle through my fingers

                      I trace one line down my body

another across

and feel filled with light

power

light as air

as I have never known

Ogie tells me that William told her it is Arbor
Day

    we spend the entire morning and afternoon
planting baby evergreens in the forest

                      halfway home
a shower overtakes us

             we wait it out on a decayed log
the rhythm of the rain drops tapping the leaves
over our heads nearly putting us to sleep

when we are home again and clean at last

we nest against each other in my bed beneath

wool blankets

                        I tongue the sharp edges

of my teeth one at a time

light a candle

turn out the lights

listening to Ogie's lullaby for William about a

lumberjack called Beckford

who roamed the earth uprooting trees

replanting them elsewhere

still beautiful

still whole

on Mother's Day

I give Ogie a crown of orange blossoms

adorned with a small pearl-dotted veil

           I have sent you an identical one

with a note to say I received your letter but do

not have a telephone so hope the gift will fit

you nicely should you ever marry again

           I add that the dusty miller

and silver sage and silver brunia I used for

filler should match your gray silk slip quite

perfectly

William watches me adjust Ogie's veil from
beyond the bedroom door

      I motion with my chin for him to join us
and he runs into Ogie's arms

      she says HOW ABOUT A MAGIC SPELL

      William nods and when immediately
it begins to rain he nearly bruises his hands
from too much clapping

      HAPPY MOTHER'S DAY William says to
Ogie

      HAPPY MOTHER'S DAY she says to me

something I don't like to think about

                              every few years

the hanged return to haunt the town

              Ogie and I tried once to talk to them

to ask if they had word of her mother

                        it was springtime

            the cherry blossoms were falling

and I couldn't bear to see them so every

morning I threw myself into the sea to try and

forget

but this made Ogie angry because I had been

ignoring her all winter

ever since she had presented herself to me on

Christmas

           she didn't care that I was trying to forget

or that it was so difficult to forget

so I ignored her

       it was easy to pretend I couldn't see her

even easier to pretend I couldn't hear her

no matter how loudly she wailed

       we passed a long winter cooped up

in the cottage

but that spring day when I came back in from

the water and acknowledged her presence on

the back porch

     YOU CAN'T IGNORE ME FOREVER

I knew something was wrong

     I NEED YOU TO TAKE ME INTO

TOWN

     THERE'S GOING TO BE A GATHERING

the rainstorms were over

the earth was still mud

we were lucky to escape

afterward

to the part of the forest where the floor of

interlocking roots was gnarled hard and nearly

too intricate to touch

we had to catch our breath

and shake off all the spirits that had joined us

all the spirits that were not her mother

all the stares of too many townspeople who

could blame only me for the trouble in their

lives

trouble they could not hear coming and could

not see

she was heartbroken and I was terrified

I had never seen so many angry ghosts

in one place

their bruised and broken necks

neither of us intended to ever return

to town during a gathering

but William tells us he is lonely and for his

birthday this is what he wants to do

> we discuss it when he is asleep

if he wants to go I don't see why you can't
take him

but in the morning THE ANSWER IS NO

he rips out his stitches

and blood falls from his cut

runs along the floor like the sun in bloom

                the room turns hot

           I leave for my morning swim

                 this is their affair

when I come home I see the wallpaper glue has

blistered and large sheets have wobbled down

in wide ribbons

                          I re-stitch William's throat

              apparently they have made their peace

and we will not be going to the gathering

                           we will instead

for the first time

celebrate Halloween

we carve a pumpkin and put it on the porch

children never come to our cottage

with the history of the place

with me never seen in town except in my black
veil

is it any surprise

I am surprised when a child knocks and
extends a scarlet pillowcase to keep her treats
in

and what are you I ask

A FREIGHTER she says

I see I say and give her a sprig of lily of
the valley

a tall man behind the child nods

his protective hands on her shoulders

and they part ways with me on the porch

                                    beneath us

under the stairs

        William and Ogie rattle chains from god

knows where and go OOH

        OOOH

        OOOOOOH

one evening William finds an emaciated bunny

in the garden

                              he names her Hindlegs

                I cradle the small animal in my arms

and bring her inside

where she laps up all the water William tells

me to put down for her

then stops with a sound of pain

                    and that is the end of Hindlegs

William wants to know where Hindlegs is

I don't know

WHERE IS SHE

WHERE DID SHE GO

I don't know

it is the same question Ogie asks about her
mother

the same question I ask about mine

    HINDLEGS IS DEAD Ogie tells him

WE ARE ALL THAT'S LEFT

it is Thanksgiving

    we light what looks to be about a thousand
candles
beautifully arranged

    Ogie wears a red bird's feather in her hair

    IT CAME FROM THE PLAINS

FELL FROM THE BRANCHES WITH A SHRIEK

DURING THE TORNADOES THAT LEFT SO MANY

DEAD THE LAND WAS HAUNTED AND ALL THE

LIVING LEFT US

we say a prayer for our bird who gobbled the
earth for us

whose remains we return to the timberline in
offering

along with his raw innards

which we bury at the base of the tallest tree

at home we have a tickling match

Ogie wins

later we take a night walk down to the sea to

watch the sky reflecting water reflecting stars

like so many unblinking

watchful eyes

                    we let out air from our mouths

rein in our first words like curls of smoke

sliding back into the throat while star patterns

glide slowly across the sky

those lights that guided sailors in the

night

spirits lost in the forest

on the first day of winter

I present Ogie with a little gift

    I have embroidered the edges of the ruffles

of her cloak with tiny golden dandelion petals

      William has a smart new three-piece suit

and a tiny top hat to match

all of it sewn in secret during his evening baths

in town we have reservations for dinner in the

restaurant of the oldest hotel

                              after my second bottle

William lifts his nose into the air and

sniffs

        Ogie says THERE ARE OTHERS HERE

                              I close my eyes

listening for the particular silence of

ghosts

like autumn leaves rustling

HELLO William says

                              I open my eyes
and see the dead man smiling down at me
peering through my veil

        LOOK WHO IT IS he says

        I REMEMBER YOU

he gestures toward the dinner stage

at a woman leaning against red velvet curtains

and asks if I remember Zepha

she puts out her cigarette

and nods at me

I nod back

there is a dinner show happening

the performers are all ghosts

I hadn't even noticed

they are taking a short break between acts

and the dead man has invited Ogie to join them

to meet the actors

                    William stays with me at the table

                                    on stage

the dead man makes introductions

and there is a lengthy discussion until Ogie

points in my direction

I bury my face in oysters

                    when I look back up

I see several more ghosts gathered around

Ogie

admiring her cloak

                         she spins

and the cloak billows out around her

         Zepha touches it and takes a step back

then inspects the seams

THEY WANT COSTUMES

AND NOT JUST COSTUMES BUT DAYCLOTHES

TOO FOR THE ONES WHO WENT THE MESSY

WAY LIKE THIS ONE

she tips her head toward William

who smiles at me wide as a melon slice

I notice

for the first time

that he is missing two molars

WE'RE IN BUSINESS NOW

we leave the restaurant with promises to

meet Ogie's new friends at the cottage in the

morning for fittings

                      we make our way home

and as we pass the old prison I stop

                      I pluck our customary rose

but before I give it to her I have to ask

you've never told me how you really died

William is asleep in Ogie's arms

                                she sets him down

against the prison's iron door

                         she pretends to shiver

                    she strokes William's hair

and he puts a finger in his mouth

        TELL ME THE TRUTH she says

                           she is stalling

ignoring my question by asking one of her own

        HAVE YOU KNOWN LOVE

perhaps from too much wine I begin to cry

          Ogie reaches to touch my cheek

but her finger goes through my veil

through the tear sliding down my face

I was kissed once

    WELL

THAT'S SOMETHING

ISN'T IT

    she brushes William's hair off his forehead

tucks a lock behind his ear

THERE WAS A LOT OF BLOOD she

says

THE LAST THING I SAW WAS WHAT A

BEAUTY SHE WAS

MY SIXTH GIRL

BORN EARLY AND SCREAMING IN MY ARMS

she touches my knee and I steel myself because

I know what she wants to know

DO YOU REMEMBER ME

I take a breath

lift my veil so I can see her face more clearly

so she can see my face more clearly

I say *yes*

I say *I do*

part three

THE TEA HOUSE

Mother did something to herself after what she
did to Grandmother

I can never speak of it
but after I saw it happen I went out back
beneath the falling cherry blossoms and buried
myself in them

I don't know why Mother did what she did but
my throat was raw for weeks after because I
had screamed so long and hard that since then
I have been able to speak in only a whisper

when the authorities came they found me

hidden beneath a blanket of fallen cherry

blossoms

unable to talk

unwilling to even whisper

going only on my appearance someone

suggested I might be rabid

                                      a noose was thrown

                          I was caught at the neck

and taken away on a long pole

subjected to needles administered in sequences

over several weeks

Mother said it was an accident and a woman

from the state became established in the cottage

the woman took care of Mother

but said I was not allowed to stay

I would have to learn to love her from afar

Mother said some things to the woman and the woman said some things to some other people who contacted the tea house

as soon as the proper papers were signed you came for me

before we left for the tea house

I brought her boiled peanuts

      I made her a grilled cheese sandwich

but these seemed only to upset her in her

darkness

you took me by the hand and tried to lead me

away

but I ran back to her

told her she was as beautiful in her red cloak as

I could remember her ever having been and in

my final whisper I said I would love her

always

the woman from the state stood beside you

dabbed her eyes

TRAGEDY she said

SHAME she said

I spent most of my time alone in the tea house
attic

       my mouth tasted constantly of metal

and I cried until I could not cry anymore

in the mornings

when you were foraging for wildflowers

you left me with your aging father

                he would look after me you said

                   you said his name was Sam

that I could trust him

as Mother trusted you

at first he tried to feed me candied oranges

but I bit him and put an end to that

                                        I was afraid

for him to touch me

               I wanted him to be afraid to touch me

every night in the tea house attic when I should

have been sleeping I plotted my return to

Mother by way of hills and town and forest

for a long time I believed she was getting better

that she would be waiting for me at the sea

still standing tall and proud

just as she had been before

as if to show me I too could square up tall and

proud

even if it is true she never wanted me and

regarded me as a mongrel

a boy mongrel at that

there is always a different version and mine is

this

                  in all our coming and going

there was only one sure thing I knew

the warmth from my own body trapped

between us as we made our way on trains and

in circuses and in the care of perfect strangers

               we were bound if not by love

together always at the leash

one afternoon

in the tea house attic

I discovered a long black mourning veil in an

antique hat box

              I began to wear it

          it helped me to remember

Mother in her darkness

I remember Mother shaved me bald one

summer when I was very young

                           someone else had been with us

in that house

but we had no choice and left

because it was filled with bats

we went by sea

        a captain who recognized Mother

and called her by name

took pity on me

gave me a coconut to play with

a few days later he took it back abruptly and
broke it

                                      he bent down
to hand me back the useless pieces that were
wet inside and lined with what I thought to be
white soap curved into rounds

some weeks later we docked

at last

and found ourselves inside the Statue of

Liberty

        for the first time I saw Mother cry

            she patted my head

which was also a first

        she seemed to be even sadder

at the sight of me

        I should have used more soap

we made our way to Central Park and I

marveled at all the people dressed in so many

shadow hues

I tried to point them out

but Mother hushed me

DO NOT SPEAK UNTIL YOU ARE SPOKEN

TO

I did not speak for years

you tried to get me to speak but I was

afraid

      you had taken me away from Mother

and I was afraid of what I might say

for the first time

I went to church

        every day I crept inside before the sun

made my way along the aisle to the first row of

pews

where I prayed for Mother

but I did not look at the crown of thorns above

me because it reminded me of the Statue of

Liberty

back at the tea house

I mended fences

                              I shined gentlemen's splats

                                  I played the piano

for the ladies having lunch

                            I learned they did not like me to play

the staccato pieces

                                      I dried dishes

and kept out of the way and never opened my

mouth

I don't know how many months passed for me
like this but at some point after all my chores
were done for the day I developed the habit of
leaving the tea house and going into the bad
parts of town to walk down dark alleys at night
to feel the thrill of fear and courage

I told no one

of course

there was no one to tell

then one day I was pitting cherries in the
kitchen

                    your husband had returned
from an extended business trip

                        he came over to me
crouched down to my level
peered closely through my veil
studying my face
and he smiled

      LOOK WHO IT IS he said

      I REMEMBER YOU

he sat himself on the counter next to the sink

     I mistrusted the sound of my own voice

but asked anyway

    are you in pain

    NO

BUT I'M STARVING

I stood and wiped my hands

retrieved a large bunch of seedless reds from

the walk-in and rinsed them for him

                         I put them in a bowl

and placed them beside him on the counter

                  I was about to tell him that lunch

would be in just a few minutes

that we were almost ready to start bringing in

the buffet trays from the dining room

and I was going to warn him that Sam always

ate the pancakes but that anything else was up

for grabs

but then I figured he probably already knew

that

BY THE WAY he said

I WAS REAL SORRY TO HEAR ABOUT YOUR

MOTHER

I sat at my place again and poked my straw

through a cherry until its pit popped out

I poked another

and its pit popped out

WHOA

HEY

LISTEN

I'M NOT TRYING TO RUIN YOUR DAY OR

ANYTHING LIKE THAT

we both turned toward the open window at the

sudden commotion from the street

HE'S BLEEDING you said

HE'S REALLY BLEEDING

then people were everywhere and everyone

was shouting orders and Sam came in and

pushed my bowls off the table and cherries and

pits spilled all over onto the floor and someone

told me

GET UP

GET OUT OF THE WAY

and they brought him in

and I scrambled and pressed myself as tightly

as I could into the farthest corner of the room

from his place on the counter he stared down at

his own remains on the kitchen table

>he turned to me and smiled again

WATCH THIS

>he reached for a grape

and his fingers went right through it

>he pretended to tug it free

tossed it into the air

craned his neck just slightly to catch it in his

open mouth

>he bit into it

then stuck out his tongue and said

SEE FOOD

                                    he laughed

and I almost laughed

but Sam came over and said

         YOU SHOULDN'T BE HERE

                        and led me gently by the arm

into the dining room

the dead man followed us out

      I'M RIGHT HERE

OKAY

                  Sam sat beside me

and held my hand

      HELP IS ON THE WAY

SO LET'S JUST STAY RIGHT HERE FOR NOW

      I nodded *okay*

they buried him on a hill of wildflowers in
simple pine

I had overheard you say you had no use
for a cemetery
the way they were made to look like gardens
with all that restriction and not enough
freedom
it would just be another heartbreak and that
you could not endure

Sam arranged to have several doves released
into the air
and you covered your heart with both hands as
they flew away

the dead man and I watched from the window

in the attic

                             when we saw everyone

making their way back down the hill

we went downstairs to greet them

   I noticed Sam's substantial nose was chapped

from too much blowing

                       he dabbed at it tenderly

with a red silk cloth

DON'T YOU THINK IT'S WONDERFUL

HOW THE LIVING COME TOGETHER TO OFFER

EACH OTHER CONDOLENCES

the dead man swiveled on the piano bench
pretended to tap a key

OH THAT LITTLE OLD WOMAN IS

PICKING GRISTLE FROM HER TEETH

I'LL BET YOU ANYTHING SHE EATS IT

I would have liked to ask him questions

but I kept myself quiet and waited until he

spoke to me

and when he did it never seemed quite right to

respond with what I thought I wanted to say

and in any case I was in and out of the tea

house clearing dishes and pouring tea and

asking if I could do anything to make anyone

more comfortable and thanking everyone for

coming and for thinking of you and of your

family in your time of need

the entire household slept poorly that night

                        I joined you in the kitchen

where you were unable to hold your little gold

scoop steady

                             I reached out

lightly wrapped two fingers and my thumb

around your wrist

let your hand guide mine in and out of various

jars of dried flowers

herbs

other ingredients

in this way

I learned the secret recipe of your personal

blend

                    I felt your pulse under my fingers

the dead man looked over our proceedings and

said

      THIS IS NUTS

      IT'S NOT LIKE I WAS MURDERED

      JUST LOOK AT ALL THESE CAKES

NOBODY ATE

          I was beginning to dislike him

but I kept it to myself

you removed your hand from mine

for the first time

I believe you really saw me and seemed happy

I was there

you took a tiny tin from your pocket

opened it

and I saw inside some substance that looked

like pink vaseline

ROSE SALVE you said

you motioned for me to sit with you at the table

where you took my hands in yours

massaged small dabs of it into the skin around

my fingernails

one at a time

then into my knuckles

all the way up to each of my wrists

THERE NOW

FEELS BETTER

DOESN'T IT

the others went to bed

       even the dead man left us alone

in the kitchen

     DO YOU REMEMBER ME you wanted to

know

     I nodded *yes*

     DO YOU REMEMBER THE WEDDING

DRESS YOUR MOTHER MADE FOR ME

     yes

DO YOU REMEMBER THE WEDDING

yes

WOULD MIND TELLING IT TO ME THE

WAY IT WAS FOR YOU

so it all spilled out
that Mother had made me a dress and I was
given the job of throwing the petals from
a basket and Sam had told me it was an
important job and I was the only one big
enough to do it and I would be the first one
anyone saw from the wedding party and
I had never been to a party and I was very
nervous about it and I was still so sorry that
I had tripped and spilled all the petals on the
steps but that it had been so nice of you to
bend down in your big dress that I thought
looked like a beautiful golden cloud to help me

scoop them back up into my basket and what I

remembered most was that you said

    DON'T CRY

    LOOK

EVERYONE IS SO HAPPY TO SEE YOU

    GO ON

THEY'RE ALL WAITING JUST FOR YOU

    and later at the dancing part

I had overheard someone say

    WITH ANY LUCK THE STORK WILL SOON

BE MAKING A DELIVERY

    so for as long as Mother and I

continued to live there

I kept watch out the window for a stork

in case anyone needed to be there to sign his

paper clipboard

you nodded and said MY HUSBAND DID
NOT WANT CHILDREN

WHEN I HEARD ABOUT YOUR MOTHER
I KNEW I WANTED YOU TO COME
BUT IT WAS STILL SO SAD FOR ME BECAUSE OF
THAT

DO YOU UNDERSTAND

I told you everything
how I kept with me the memory of the warmth
and smell of your delicious stews you only
made on rainy days when you had the time to
let them cook and cook because all the other
days you were out among the wildflowers
every morning without fail
how I loved and had always remembered the
tall white pitchers you filled with elaborate
arrangements that you seemed able to make

like magic from simple decisions of this
wildflower or that wildflower
and I told you that I remembered thinking the
very rooms and the wildflowers in them were
even happier when you were in them too

                                               I told you
I remembered how you had sat at the piano
with me every evening after dinner to teach me
the songs my fingers never forgot
not even after so many years away
and I said it was strange to think about how
the body holds memories in its parts and that I
wondered what other memories my body held
without my even knowing it

                                     we were silent for a time
and then you confessed that for many years
your husband had been having an affair with a
woman named Zepha
but then Zepha had died from esophageal
cancer and your husband had been very sad for

many weeks until finally doing what he did

you said that on the one hand
his death was a tragedy and for that reason you
were in mourning but on the other hand you
felt very numb to it all because you had never
really loved him

you said you felt guilty
more than anything
because you had always considered it a
convenience that he traveled so much for
business

you asked me
then if I would give you a few minutes alone if
you went upstairs to bed and in a little while
would I bring up a glass of water

when I went upstairs

I saw you had taken off your dress

you were sitting on the edge of your bed

in only a gray silk slip

I tried to hand you the water

but you asked me to put it on the table and

when I reached over you lifted my veil and

kissed me on the mouth

I heard the water glass fall and break

          I felt your tongue on my tongue

               I felt your nails

press into the undersides of my hands

        I smelled vanilla and cinnamon smoke

in your hair from Sam's evening pipe

I thought of all I had ever heard about lovers
and tried to understand what it meant to be in
someone's bedroom and at the same time feel
somewhere else

your fingers grazed the sides of my neck

and I felt your palms under my jaw

the pressure of your thumbs on my cheeks

your fingertips in my hair

     I rested my own hands on your shoulders

and when the straps of your slip fell away you

began to sob

fell back onto the bed

waved for me to leave the room

I passed the dead man on my way out

HOW LONG HAS THIS BEEN GOING ON

I lowered my veil and ran

it was not until early the next day that I was able to finally fall asleep but no one disturbed me and when I woke that afternoon and made my way downstairs and through the house to the kitchen where I found my lunch waiting I saw someone else had performed my morning chores the next few days were hot and clouded

                      the air felt gritty on my skin

           the dead man trailed me wherever I went

           eventually I said *whatever it is you need to*

say

say it

           he said WILL YOU TELL HER SOMETHING

FOR ME

           TELL HER I REGRET THAT I WAS NOT A

VERY GOOD HUSBAND

AND I'M SORRY

why did you marry her

he made a suck sound

with his tongue on a tooth

I LOVED HER

but then you didn't anymore

YEAH

SOMETHING LIKE THAT

because there had been so many family

members in attendance at the funeral

you took the opportunity to gather your

remaining living relatives into small groups for

pictures

in every photograph I was caught in

the image of me was always beside a sunburst

the shape of the dead man

Sam wondered aloud

if I had a chemical imbalance

I felt a tickling sensation crawl up my back

I knew if I told the truth

there might be consequences

even though I thought it cruel to keep

them from the knowledge of the dead man's

presence in their lives

and particularly of his regret

I stirred my tea leaves and said I didn't

understand

TAKE THAT OFF you said

AND LOOK AT ME

I lifted my veil and looked at you

and when I looked away

you said I'M SORRY

                                        I stood there

face burning

and watched you leave the room

I tried to explain but as the days and weeks

went by we forgot all about it until one Sunday

when we were closed for spring cleaning

          we were covered in a thin layer of filth

but we were happy

                              you were singing

and everything beyond the windows was

blossoms and blankets of sunshine and sky

and that's when a tall woman arrived and said

her name was Zepha

she looked hungry

so I put down a plate of cookies for her

and she pretended to help herself

DO YOU MIND IF I SMOKE

I HATE THE TASTE BUT IT HELPS MY

NERVES

then she said I JUST WANT HER TO

KNOW THAT I LOVED HIM

I STILL DO

AND NOW I WOULD LIKE TO TAKE HIM WITH

ME

AWAY FROM HERE

that night we went up the hill

to the dead man's grave

      the moon above us was round as a coin

            we stayed at his grave

until the wind settled

and I knew then that the dead man was no

longer your husband but Zepha's

and we made our way home

the years passed us quietly by

but our routines remained steady as ever

every spring we cleaned

and in the summers we chased flies from the

kitchen

every autumn

we prepared the house for winter

which is when I was invited to learn the secrets

of your recipes

it seemed we could fill the entire house

with scent and steam

and soon I was able to seal the sachets with

the precise quantities of leaves and herbs and

flowers almost as well as you and your mother

and your grandmother

still I grew weary

                                 occasionally

I found myself at the attic window

staring out over the white hills

dreaming of stepping out in a fine dress from

the tallest of all tall buildings onto a busy street

where people parted ways for me to walk

cleanly through

often I dreamed of the sea and how it rises in a
storm
how it sets free the smells of the earth

all of this was to escape the fact that Sam had

become incapable

                      you could hardly bear it

so I added the tending of his body to my daily

chores

on my 18th birthday it rained late into the night

and into the next morning

after several days

the basement flooded

then the yard

and you worried for the rest of the house

until one morning the sun returned

the world turned bright

newly shined

and we discovered on the porch some dozen

wooden crates screwed tight and addressed to

me

I worked at the screws and the wet wooden

sides fell away from their frames

their inner walls were lined

with thickly padded red crushed velvet

one after another

they revealed hundreds of Mother's dresses

beside me you shook your head

WHAT ARE YOU SUPPOSED TO DO WITH

EMPTY CRATES

there was a note

AFTER MANY YEARS I HAVE COLLECTED
THEM ALL WITH TWO EXCEPTIONS A NEEDLE
LACE WEDDING DRESS IN THE ATTIC OF THE
TEA HOUSE YOU RESIDE IN CURRENTLY AND A
RED CLOAK IN THE CLOSET OF THE COTTAGE
YOU NOW OWN WHICH YOU ARE FREE TO
RETURN TO AT ANY TIME

YOUR MOTHER'S FRIEND

CHARLOTTE

I said I would never leave you

        I said Sam needed me too much

      I said I needed you and Sam too much

the two of you were my only family

          but you were unyielding

       the arrival of the crates worried you

because their mysterious appearance made my

appearance more mysterious

more noticeable

      you told me I no longer needed you

that Charlotte was looking out for me now

         you told me to go home

I was unprepared for the open ache that fell on
top of me as I made the long walk down Prison
Lane

it was even worse
when I unlocked the cottage door

I was so lonely
lonely for you
lonely all over again for Mother
haunted by the absences of everyone I had ever
loved
all the empty space they could have filled
even Charlotte
who remained and is still untraceable

my first night alone in the cottage

after the sun went down

I made a cup of your blend from the ribbon-

wrapped bundle of sachets you pressed into

my palms before I left

                          I couldn't sleep

                 the cottage was so empty

all my aching erupted to the surface

I remembered that day all over again

the cherry blossoms were in bloom

I stepped out from under them

to look up at the sky and in an instant I was

drenched

the rain came and went

and the sky turned a deep dark violet

I took myself inside

to change out of my wet clothes

I could not get to her in time

   all I could do was run to her and scream

    I screamed as I held her in my arms

   I screamed as I tried to remove the scissors

    I screamed when Ogie came toward me

and tried to hold me in her arms

    I screamed when she tried to remove

the scissors but couldn't because her hands

went through the handles

I ran back outside

back into the safety of the cherry blossoms

clutching and clawing at my broken throat

believing I had lost my mind

Mother said I HEARD A GIRL SCREAM

ONCE

                       we were outside in chairs

just the two of us

          the woman from the state was inside

behind the window's glass

                we had blankets in our laps

and Mother was wearing her cloak

                   an afterstorm sprinkle

fell onto our upturned faces

           we listened to the wind in the trees

she said RAIN SILL LIGHTNING SWEAT

she told me the story

of how I came to be

I HAD NEVER SEEN A BEING BEAUTIFUL

AS YOU

I knew she did not mean me

but to hear her tell it that way

to hear her say YOU

it was nearly as good as

then the woman from the state came out

and asked what I would like to drink

Mother said MAY I HAVE COCOA

PLEASE

then she finished her story

PETALS

DEAD BREAST

LAWN

in the morning we were gone
you took me away
and spoke of shadow memories
you said I would always have them
that I would always carry them with me
no matter how far away they were

and then you wrapped me in your arms

and said GIVE ME YOUR PAIN

I CAN TAKE IT

I WILL TAKE IT

epilogue

it is the end of a beautiful fall

                    the changing of the leaves

has been a gorgeous drama reenacted on the

stage at the dinner theatre by the ghost actors

and actresses I have fitted and dressed and

housed and fed this past year with materials

from Mother's crates

tonight

in anticipation of winter

I light our fiery oven and spread fresh butter on

a slice of crusty sunflower bread

outside

the last of the roses writhe in a wind and cling

to the earth

                         William goes to bed

and Ogie falls asleep on her recliner

                    I pour myself a glass of wine

and sit at the window

where her mother sat

and where my mothers before me tended the

task of living in this cottage by the sea

listen

if you should ever need us

our windows are lit with candles

the door is open

acknowledgements

Thank you to the following readers who
helped shape this book in its earliest drafts:
Lucy Biederman, Sue Bottigheimer, Doug Paul
Case, Kathy Fish, Jamie Iredell, Brittany Jacoby,
Alyse Knorr, Michael Lee, Amy Minton,
Elizabeth Deanna Morris, Kadzi Mutizwa, Ben
Segal, Brooke Shaffner, J. A. Tyler, Michael
Joseph Walsh, Joel Whitney. Special thanks to
Kirsten Bakis, for the late night talks.

Thank you also to the following editors who
published excerpts from *Desire: A Haunting*,
and/or under various working titles *Ogie: A
Biography* and *Ogie: A Ghost Story*: Amanda Earl
at *Experiment-O*; Tantra Bensko at *Lucid Play*;
Cynthia Reeser at *Prick of the Spindle*; David
Blumenshine at *Similar:Peaks*::; Dena Rash
Guzman at *Unshod Quills*; Alyse Knorr at *Sugar
Mule*; Zach Doss at *Black Warrior Review*.

And finally, thank you to J.A. Tyler, who first
midwifed *We Take Me Apart* into the world,
without whom there would be no dog or Ogie.
Best for last, deepest thanks to Jason Cook —
editor, publisher, friend.

about the author

Molly Gaudry is the author of *We Take Me Apart*, which was shortlisted for the PEN/ Joyce Osterweil and a finalist for the Asian American Literary Award for Poetry. Find her at mollygaudry.com.

www.ingramcontent.com/pod-product-compliance
Lightning Source LLC
Chambersburg PA
CBHW021407110726
47901CB00008B/2086